The See-saw

Written by Paul Shipton
Illustrated by Brett Hudson

Collins

The monkey went up.

The crocodile went up.

The lion went up.

The mouse went up.

The hippo went up.

The mouse went down.

13

A Flowchart

14

☁️ Ideas for guided reading ☁️

Learning objectives: talk about patterns in a story; hear and say phonemes in initial letters; match spoken and written words; ask and answer questions and offer suggestions.

Curriculum links: Mathematical Development: using words like 'heavier/lighter' to compare quantities; Knowledge and Understanding of the World: Why things happen and how things work

High frequency words: up, went, the, and, down

Interest words: see-saw, monkey, crocodile, lion, mouse, hippo, animals

Word count: 24

Resources: plastic model animals, rulers, cotton reels

Getting started

- Ask the children to look carefully at the front cover and predict the title.
- Read the question in the blurb. Walk through the pictures of the book up to p13, discussing what is happening. On p2, ask the children to find the word *went* and ask what sound it starts with.
- On p2, model correct matching of words and spoken sounds.

Reading and responding

- Ask the children to read the book aloud from the beginning. As the children read, prompt and praise correct matching of spoken and written words.
- Ask them to say what happens to the see-saw when each animal gets on. *How many animals will it take to make the hippo go up?*
- Discuss the pattern of words on each page. *When does it change?* Can the children find the same words on different pages?
- Look together at the flow chart on pp14–15 and discuss the story. Ask why the see-saw doesn't move at first. *What happens when each animal sits on the see-saw?* Discuss which animal is lightest and which is heaviest.